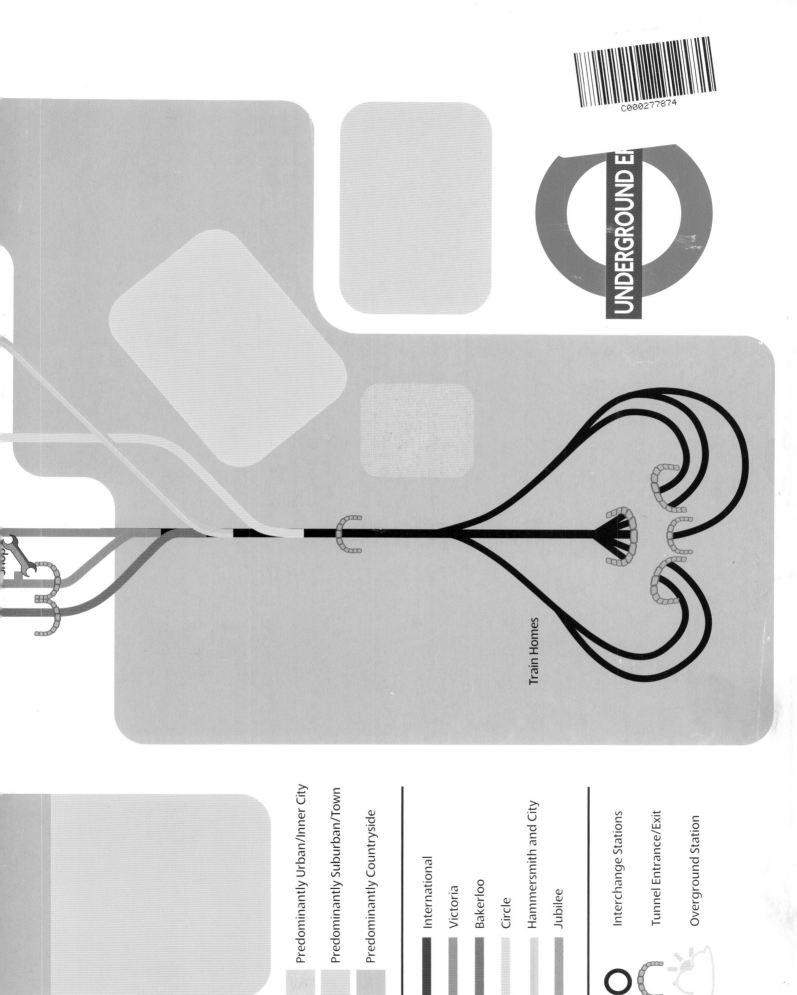

Train Homes

UNDERGROUND E

Predominantly Urban/Inner City

Predominantly Suburban/Town

Predominantly Countryside

International

Victoria

Bakerloo

Circle

Hammersmith and City

Jubilee

Interchange Stations

Tunnel Entrance/Exit

Overground Station

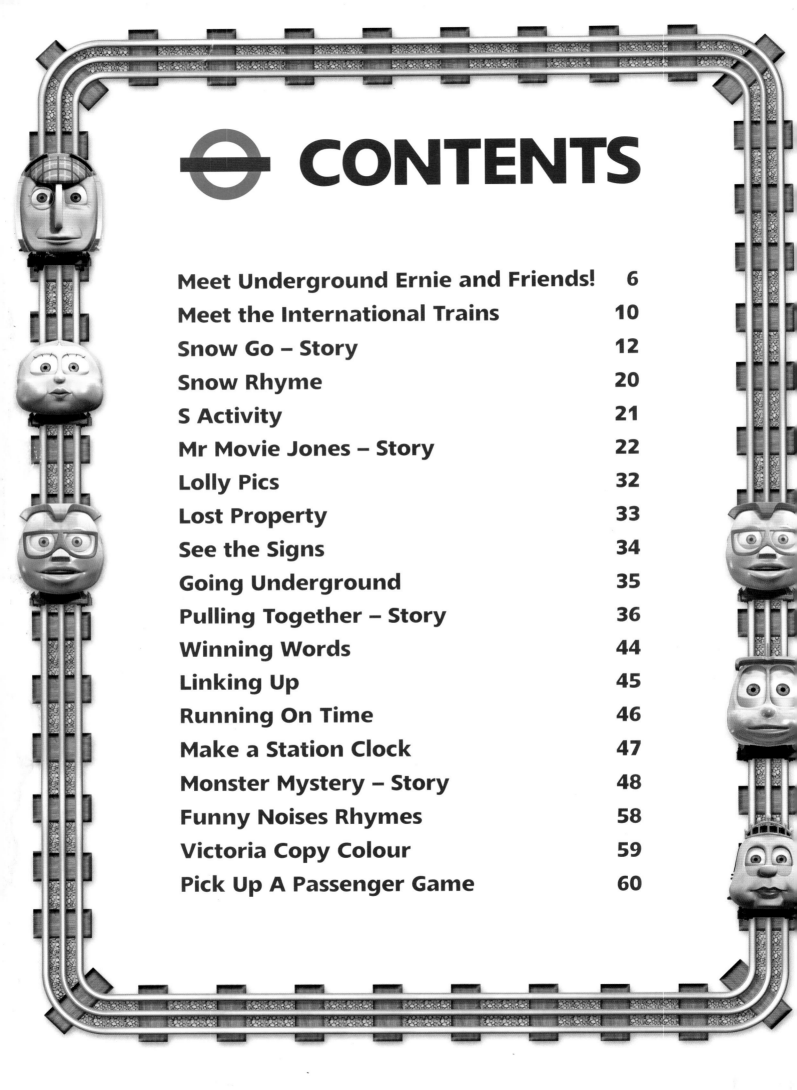

CONTENTS

UNDERGROUND ERNIE ™

Pedigree®

Published by Pedigree Books Limited
Beech Hill House, Walnut Gardens, Exeter, Devon EX4 4DH.

E-mail books@pedigreegroup.co.uk

Published 2006

£6.99

Meet Underground Ernie and Friends

Ernie

Ernie is the jolly, kind-hearted supervisor of International Underground. His job is to keep things running smoothly so that his passengers arrive safely and on time. He loves to be up and about early in the morning and says that early risers have more fun!

UNDERGROUND ERNIE

ERNIE 1

Millie

Computer expert Millie operates the control desk in the office at International Station. She loves to travel and goes somewhere exciting every weekend on one of the international trains. She always brings back interesting souvenirs from her trips!

Mr Rails

No job is too big or too small for maintenance man Mr Rails. Whether he's clearing rubbish, repairing trains, or is in his workshop, he does it with a smile. In his many years of working on the Underground, his motto has always been 'Mr Rails never fails!'

Bakerloo

Clever Bakerloo is the Sherlock Holmes of the Underground, never happier than when he is playing detective and solving a mystery. Although grumpy at times, no problem is too great for him and he often gets Ernie out of tricky situations.

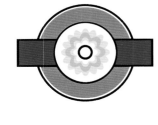

Circle

This laid-back hippy-chick is a gentle and friendly train. Circle sees beauty in everything around her and never loses her cool or raises her soft voice. She is always willing to help Ernie and the other trains whenever she can.

Jubilee

Jubilee is the youngest of the trains. He's gadget mad and is into computer games, the internet and music. His energy and curiosity sometimes get him into trouble with the older trains, but they know at heart that International Underground would be dull without him!

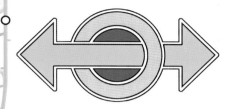

Hammersmith and City

These fast and furious twins go to and from the city, arguing happily and always trying to outsmart each other. They both love sport and have the stadium on their line, but they support different football teams, of course: the Reds are Hammersmith's team, while City supports the Blues. Find out what happens when their teams play against each other in 'Pulling Together'!

Victoria

Victoria is the warm-hearted grandmother of International Underground. She has some great stories to tell and often entertains the other trains with tales of bygone days. Despite her age, she isn't stuffy and is quite happy to join in the football songs on match day!

Meet the International Trains

Moscow

Moscow has to be tough and strong to take passengers during the Russian winter, so he's a great help when snow needs clearing from the tracks. He makes Ernie laugh with his mixed-up sayings, such as when he promises to 'fly like the windows!'

Brooklyn

Straight-talking Brooklyn often comes into International Station all the way from the US of A! He loves to see Ernie and friends and once spent the day with Circle to find out what life was like on a different line for a change.

Paris

Running on time is very important to Paris. He likes a tidy carriage too, so he always reminds his passengers to take their belongings with them. Thanks to Paris, Ernie can now speak a few words of French!

Sydney

Even when Sydney has just done the long journey from Australia, she always has a bright and cheerful 'G'day, guys!' for her friends. Like any surf-loving Aussie, she likes to relax between trips by the beach at Seashell Bay.

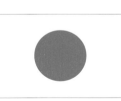

Osaka

Jubilee really looks forward to Osaka's visits, because he knows that his Japanese friend will bring the latest gadgets for him to try! Osaka is famous for his speed: he's the fastest train on International Underground!

Snow Go

It was a wintry afternoon and Ernie was waiting for the arrival of Moscow the Russian train at International Station.

"Brrr!" he shivered, rubbing his hands and stamping his feet to get warm. "I've never known it so c-c-cold!"

At last Moscow arrived, bringing champion skaters Sasha and Natasha for the following day's ice skating competition. Ernie and Millie gave the couple a warm welcome as they stepped off their train.

"Jubilee will take you straight to your hotel," Ernie told them.

"You'd better hurry, Jubilee," said Millie. "Snow is forecast for tonight."

"Yippee!" grinned Jubilee. He loved snow!

The first snowflakes began to fall that evening. Circle's last stop was the Nature Reserve.

"Oh, Pippa," she sighed, "isn't the snow beautiful?"

"Yes, Circle," Pippa agreed, "but I'm worried about keeping the animals warm."

Circle promised to bring some extra straw the next morning and headed to her shed for the night. Bakerloo, meanwhile, was at Mystery Mansion.

"Ugh! Horrible, white shivery stuff," he complained. Alice told him not to be so grumpy.

"The snow's fun!" she teased, locking the tower. Bakerloo did not think so.

"It freezes up my workings and causes nothing but trouble," he scowled.

When the trains came out of their sheds the next morning, they were astonished to find they could barely move forward an inch through the thick snow.

"We're stuck!" exclaimed Bakerloo. "We could be trapped for weeks!"

"But it's the ice skating competition today!" said Hammersmith.

"And I need to take Pippa some extra straw to keep the animals warm," added Circle.

"Victoria to Millie," Victoria called on her radio. "We're snowed in at the sheds!"

Millie told the trains not to panic.

"When there's trouble on the tracks," she said, "there's only one thing to do."

"Ask Ernie!" chorused the trains.

Moscow was
the only train out
on the tracks: he was used
to snow and was puzzled to find International
Station empty.

"The others are trapped at the sheds," Ernie explained. "I've hundreds of passengers and no trains to take them anywhere."

"Do not worry, my friend," boomed Moscow. "I will clear the tracks for you."

"Really?" said Ernie.

"Of course," chuckled Moscow. "I am tough and strong. How you say...as fit as a fishcake, yes?"

Ernie smiled as Moscow sped off to make sure Sasha and Natasha got to the ice skating competition on time.

Mr Rails did not mind the cold either. He skied merrily towards the sheds with his spades, before hitting a bank and somersaulting head first into the snow.

"Morning!" he grinned, pulling himself up and brushing away the snow. Ernie joined him and they worked hard to clear the tracks, with extra help from Alice.

"Link up, City," said Hammersmith, once the tracks were clear. "We need to hurry if we're going to see the ice skating competition!"

"I'm right behind you," called City.

Circle hurried off to the Nature Reserve and Victoria sped away to take extra blankets to the hospital.

"I must go and buy some cool snow goggles!" exclaimed Jubilee, setting off eagerly. "I mean, I must pick up my passengers from the airport..."

Bakerloo shivered and shrank back into his shed.

"What about you, Bakerloo?" asked Ernie.

"You're taking me back to Mystery Mansion, aren't you?" smiled Alice, climbing aboard.

"Oh, very well," grumbled Bakerloo. "But don't blame me if my tubes freeze up!"

Once the trains had left, Mr Rails gathered up his spades.

"More digging, Mr Rails?" asked Ernie.

"Ah, now that would be telling..." replied Mr Rails with a twinkle in his eye.

Ernie was very happy that International Underground was running normally again. When he went back to International Station later, he saw Moscow there.

"Mission accomplished, Ernie," said the Russian train. "Every track is clear."

"And guess what?" called Hammersmith, arriving back from the sports stadium. "Sasha and Natasha won their competition!"

The delighted skaters stepped on to the platform, wearing gold medals round their necks.

"Oh, marvellous!" said Moscow. "This is the ice cream on my cake, yes?"

"I couldn't have put it better myself, Moscow," chuckled Ernie, waving goodbye as the skaters began their long journey back to Russia.

The trains were glad to get back to their sheds that night.

"I think the snow looks beautiful," sighed Circle, "twinkling like a thousand diamonds."

"Well, I'm happy that Dr Heart's hospital patients are snug and warm," said Victoria.

"And I will be soon," added Bakerloo. "I'm going to put my heater on full blast and...oh!" Bakerloo had been hit by a snowball!

"Who's for a snowball fight?" chuckled Ernie, peeping from behind a tree.

The trains cheered as Ernie, Millie and Mr Rails ran to and fro, throwing snowballs at the trains and each other.

Even Bakerloo began to smile!

 Snow!

"It's horrible, white shivery stuff!" says grumpy Bakerloo,

But Circle thinks it's beautiful, and City loves it, too!

Jubilee exclaims "Yippee!" and Hammersmith shouts "Wow!"

They'd like to see a snowman but Victoria says, "Not now.

We have to take our passengers, these lines need to be clear."

Mr Rails skis up with spades, and soon Ernie is here.

They clear the tracks and Moscow helps; they get a tough job done.

Then Ernie smiles, "Snow's not all bad – a snowball fight is fun!"

⊖ 'S' For Snow!

Mr Rails skied to the trains to help dig them out of the snow. *Ski* and *snow* both begin with the 's' sound. Use a pen or pencil to draw a circle around the other things on this page that begin with the 's' sound. What sound do the other things begin with? The answers are at the bottom of the page.

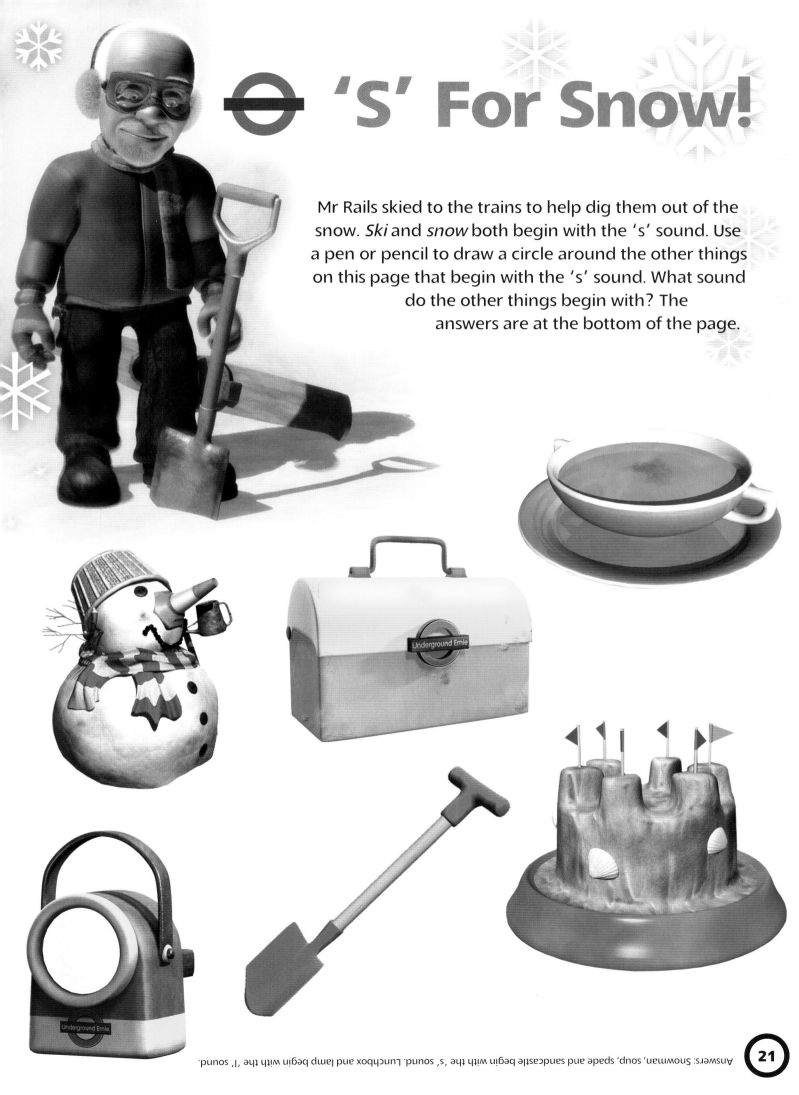

Answers: Snowman, soup, spade and sandcastle begin with the 's' sound. Lunchbox and lamp begin with the 'l' sound.

Mr Movie Jones

It was a special day at Seashell Station: a very important visitor was due to arrive.

Mr Rails was tidying up. "I don't know – the rubbish people drop!" he grumbled.

Ernie arrived. "Hello, Mr Rails," he smiled. "Are you all ready for our film director?"

"Nearly," replied Mr Rails. "This is the last bagful of rubbish to go on the trailer."

"Excellent," said Ernie. "I do hope Mr Movie Jones makes his next film here."

"So we could be in the movies?" asked Mr Rails.
"You never know," chuckled Ernie.

"I could be a pirate," said Mr Rails, grabbing a hat from the shop. "Ahaaar!"

Mr Rails began to move his trailer, but one of the rubbish bags dropped off it.

"Mr Rails, stop!" shouted Ernie, but another bag fell on to the platform and split.

Mr Rails turned to see the mess. "Ohh!" he groaned, as he heard Circle approaching.

They sighed with relief when none of the passengers looked like the film director.

Circle smiled at Mr Rails' hat. "I was practising for Mr Movie Jones," he explained.

"Well, he won't be impressed," said Circle. "The station looks like a rubbish dump!"

Ernie had a plan. He called Millie on his way back to International Station.

"Keep Mr Movie Jones away from Sea Shell Bay," he said. "Rightio," agreed Millie.

Ernie said the director was sure to be in a suit and sunglasses. Bakerloo spotted him.

The man asked to go to Seashell Bay, so Bakerloo knew he must be Mr Movie Jones.

"Tell Ernie not to worry," Bakerloo told Millie. "Mr Movie Jones is on board!"

Bakerloo took a detour to Mystery Mansion to give Mr Rails time to clean up.

"But I want to go to the seaside!" the man said crossly, striding back on to Bakerloo.

Bakerloo took him to International Station. "I want to get to Seashell Bay!" he cried.

"Hop on to Jubilee," Ernie said calmly, leading him aboard. "He knows the way."

Jubilee stopped at Shoppers' Paradise. "This isn't Seashell Bay either!" the man exclaimed.

"Right, I'll call a taxi," he said. "Stop!" called Jubilee. "I'll take you right away!"

Mr Rails had cleaned up at last, helped by a passenger. "Thanks, Mr...er," he began.

"Just call me Charlie," smiled the passenger, as Circle pulled into the station again.

"Oh, the station's all clean and tidy again," smiled Circle. "You've done a fab job!"

Jubilee brought his passenger back. "Now he's really grumpy," he warned Ernie.

"This way for the seaside, sir," Millie smiled, leading the man to Circle.

As soon as he arrived, the man unfolded a chair and sat down with a sigh.

Ernie was puzzled. "Er, Mr Movie Jones...would you like to look around?" he asked.

"I'm not Mr Movie Jones," scoffed the man. "My name's Colin Wilson!"

"I'm on holiday," he added. "So where's the real Mr Movie Jones?" asked Ernie.

"That's me," Charlie said brightly. "You?" gasped Ernie and Mr Rails.

Charlie nodded. "And I've decided that Sea Shell Bay will be perfect for my film."

"So you need a star actor?" Mr Rails asked hopefully. "A handsome, charming man?"

"Of course," said Charlie. "Ernie, you have star quality. Is it Hollywood for you?"

Ernie was surprised. "Me?" he gasped. "Gosh! I'll, er, have a think about it..."

Ernie quickly decided he didn't want to be a film star and the trains were pleased.

"Ernie would never leave us," said Victoria, that night. "He loves his job too much!"

Lolly Pics

Mr Rails picked up all sorts of rubbish at Seashell Bay, including ice-lolly sticks! Save your lolly sticks instead of throwing them away and you can make a little photo frame with them.

All you need are:
8 straight lolly sticks (make sure they're clean!)
Safe glue
Paint or felt-tips
Round-ended scissors
Thin card (such as from a cereal box)
A photo
A grown-up!

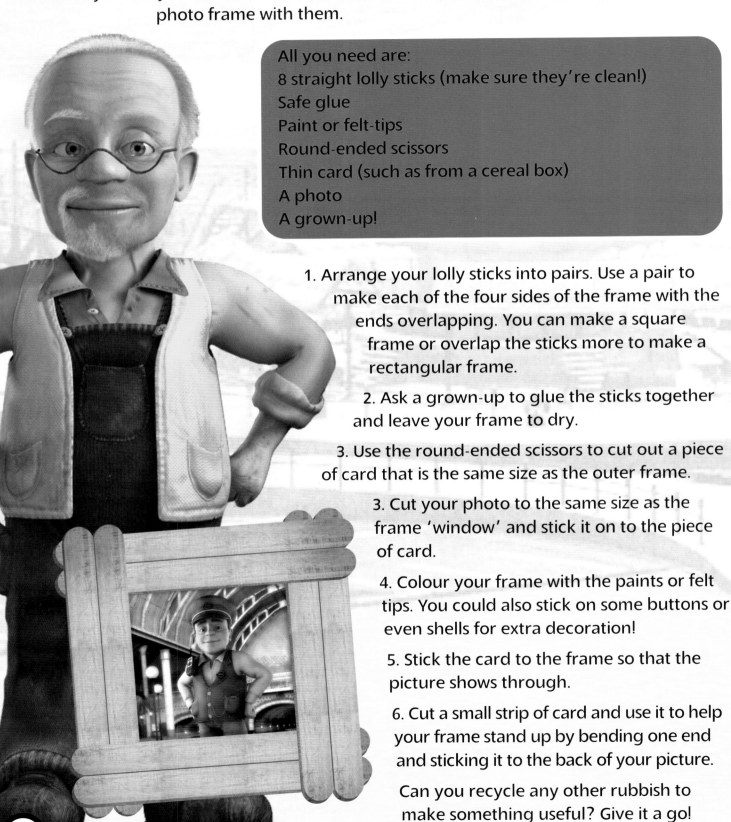

1. Arrange your lolly sticks into pairs. Use a pair to make each of the four sides of the frame with the ends overlapping. You can make a square frame or overlap the sticks more to make a rectangular frame.

2. Ask a grown-up to glue the sticks together and leave your frame to dry.

3. Use the round-ended scissors to cut out a piece of card that is the same size as the outer frame.

3. Cut your photo to the same size as the frame 'window' and stick it on to the piece of card.

4. Colour your frame with the paints or felt tips. You could also stick on some buttons or even shells for extra decoration!

5. Stick the card to the frame so that the picture shows through.

6. Cut a small strip of card and use it to help your frame stand up by bending one end and sticking it to the back of your picture.

Can you recycle any other rubbish to make something useful? Give it a go!

Lost Property

Mr Rails is always amazed at the things people leave behind on the station platforms! Look at the lost property he has picked up this week. Use a pencil to match up the pairs and draw a circle around the one left over.

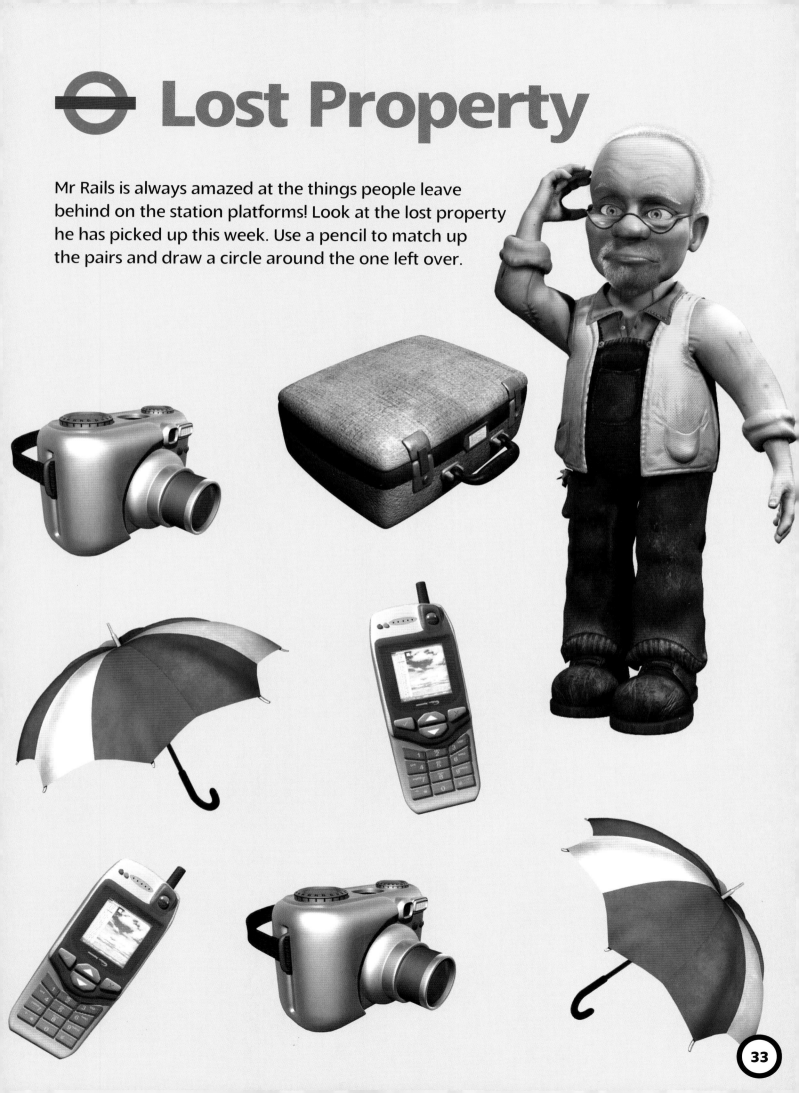

See the Signs

Each of Ernie's trains has its own line and its own sign, too! Use a pencil to match Victoria, Circle and Jubilee to their special signs.

Going Underground

If you had your own line on Ernie's International Underground, what would you call it? What sort of stations would you like on it? When you have thought of a name for your line, design your own sign for it below. Make it a colourful one!

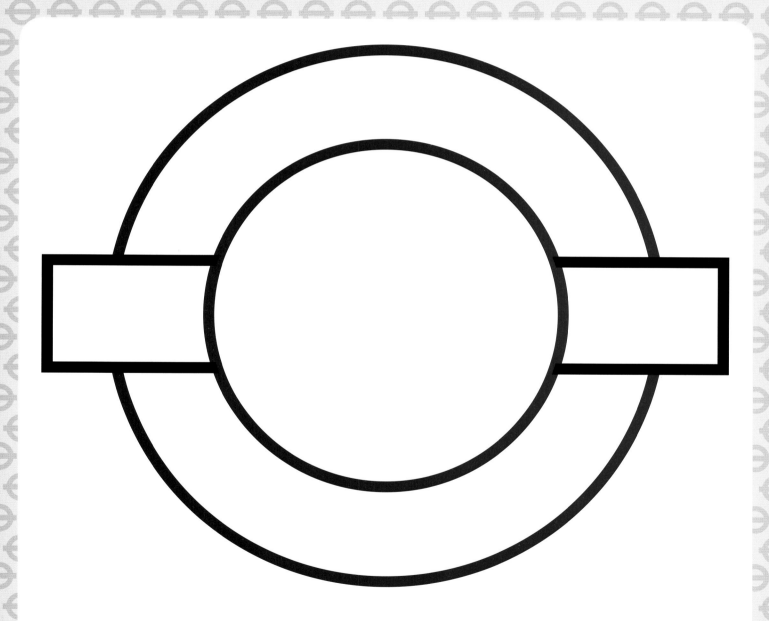

The name of my line is:

Pulling Together

It was cup match day and International Station was full of football fans.

"I've never seen the platforms so crowded," said Ernie, coming into the office. He was wearing a red rosette and a blue one.

"Can't you decide which team to support, Ernie?" asked Millie. Ernie wanted both teams to win.

"The manager of the Underground can't take sides," he explained.

While Millie asked Victoria to help Hammersmith and City with all their passengers, Ernie found his binoculars.

"I'll be at the Sports Stadium Station," he told Millie. "Someone needs to keep an eye on things."

"Of course, it's all under control" Millie smiled.

Hammersmith and City loved football, too.

"2, 4, 6, 8!" chanted Hammersmith, as they sped along.

"Which team do we think is great?" added City.

"The Reds!" sang Hammersmith.

"The Blues!" City sang louder.

They pulled into International Station to pick up more fans and found Bakerloo looking puzzled as to what was going on. Hammersmith explained that people were going to watch the match.

"I don't like football," Bakerloo said. "It makes friends fall out."

"Oh, we'd never fall out over a silly football match, would we, Hammersmith?" City insisted and his twin agreed. Bakerloo was not so sure...

Hammersmith and City were upset when Ernie told them they were on duty that afternoon.

"But we've been looking forward to the match all week!" protested City.

"Well, I'll make sure you get to parade the winning team around the Underground," said Ernie. "How about that?"

"As long as it's the Reds," agreed Hammersmith.

"As long as it's the Blues!" City insisted.

The twins dashed between stations, hoping that they might catch the second half of the match. Millie had to tell them to slow down.

"You're not giving your passengers time to get on and off!" she scolded.

When Jubilee saw Hammersmith and City back at International Station, they were still hurrying around.

"What's the rush?" he asked. City told him that they wanted to get back to the Sports Stadium for the football.

"Oh, I've been following that match on the internet," said Jubilee.

"Really?" asked Hammersmith. "What's the score?" Before pulling away,

Jubilee told them that the score was one-nil.

"To which team?" the twins called after him, but he was disappearing into the tunnel. The pair began to quarrel about which team must be winning.

"Do stop arguing," Millie told them.

"I'll ask Ernie."

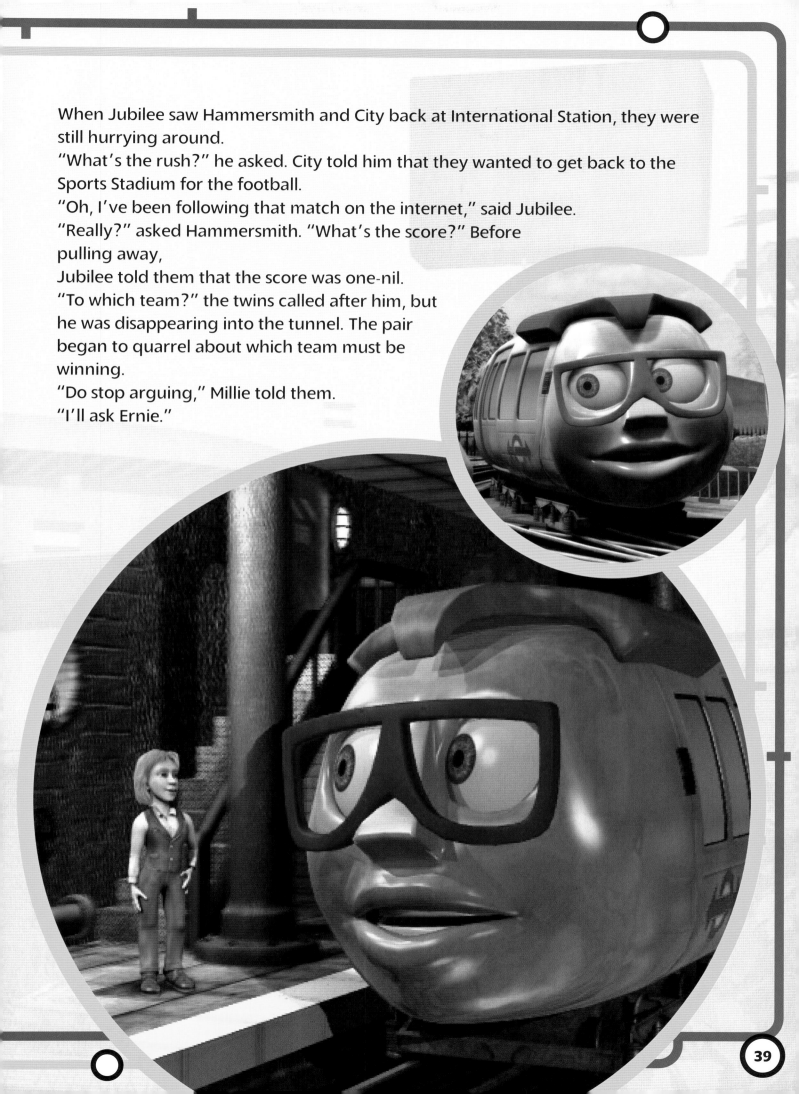

Ernie was watching the game through his binoculars from the station and told Millie that the Reds were winning.

"Yes!" cheered Hammersmith when he heard the news. "2, 4, 6, 8, which team do we know is great? THE REDS! One nil, one nil, one nil, one nil..."

"Stop it, Hammersmith," snapped City, but his twin carried on chanting.

"If you don't stop," he warned, "I'll put on my brakes." Still Hammersmith teased him. There was a nasty SCR-R-REEECH! as City carried out his threat and his twin tried to keep going. Suddenly, SNAP! Hammersmith and City came apart!

"Now look what you've done!" gasped Hammersmith.

"It wasn't my fault," sniffed City. Hammersmith called Millie for help and soon Ernie was beside them with Mr Rails.

"So, how did this happen?" asked Ernie, while Mr Rails began to repair the trains. Hammersmith explained that it was City's fault, but City said it was Hammersmith's fault for going on about the Reds winning.

"Now twins, you're supposed to be pulling together, not apart," Ernie said sternly. The pair thought for a moment and realised Ernie was right.

"Sorry, Hammersmith," said City.

"Sorry, City," said Hammersmith.

"Sorry, Ernie," they said together.

"There, all fixed and ready to go," smiled Mr Rails. "Mr Rails never fails!"

Hammersmith and City thanked Mr Rails and hurried to the stadium for the end of the match. They pulled up next to Victoria, who was happily joining in the football songs in her high singing voice.

"What's the score, Victoria?" asked Hammersmith.

"Well, the Reds were sitting pretty," she replied, "but at the end of the day, the Blues put the ball in the back of the net. So, I'm over the moon because they've both won."

"I think she means it's a draw," chuckled Hammersmith.

"I heard that the Reds and the Blues are replaying their match next Saturday," Jubilee said that night.

"Yes. Ernie said we could watch it this time," said Hammersmith.

"As long as we stay friends," added City.

"So who will parade the winning team around the Underground?" asked Circle. The twins began to argue again about whether they would parade the Reds or the Blues.

"Perhaps I should take that job," interrupted Victoria.

"You, Victoria?" asked Bakerloo.

"Yes," she nodded. "We work as a team, remember? Now, sing with me: we all agree that working together is magic!"

Winning Words

Look at these words from the story and see if you can find them in the wordsearch square. The words read across, down, forwards and backwards.

BLUES   **MATCH**   **SCORE**   **TEAMS**
CITY   **REDS**   **SONGS**   **TRAINS**

```
T R A I N S S
E J Y T I C
A R E D S O
M A T C H R
S G N O S E
F S E U L B
```

Spot the Difference

Mr Rails was so dirty after putting Hammersmith and City back together, he made Ernie and Millie laugh! If you look carefully, there are 5 differences between these pictures, can you spot them all?

Answers: 1. Ernie's Badge is missing from his jacket. 2. Mr Rails' jacket is now green. 3. Millie has 2 pockets on her jacket. 4. There is a red spade next to Mr Rails. 5. There is snow outside!

Running on Time

Ernie likes his international trains to run on time. Paris especially cannot bear to be late! Show Ernie what time these trains are due to arrive at International Underground Station today by drawing the right time on each clock.

Sydney is due to arrive at 2 o'clock.

Osaka is due to arrive at 10 o'clock.

Paris is due to arrive at 5 o'clock.

Brooklyn is due to arrive at 8 o'clock

⊖ The Station Clock

You can make your own station clock to practise telling the time with!

All you need are:

A paper plate	Paints (preferably	Round-ended scissors
A split pin	red and blue)	A grown-up!
Thin card	A dark felt-tip pen	

1. First paint your paper plate. You can paint it in the Underground colours if you like: paint a blue strip right across the middle, then use red paint to colour in the plate's rim.

2. When the paint has dried, ask a grown-up to help you write in the numbers with your felt-tip. Put the 12, 3, 6 and 9 in first, then add the numbers in between.

3. Ask your grown-up to draw you a big hand and a small hand on the thin card. Cut them out with the round-ended scissors.

4. Put the hands together and ask a grown up to fix them to the centre of the plate, using the split pin. The hands should be secure enough to stay in place, but easy to move.

Now try out some train times. All aboard!

Monster Mystery

One morning, the trains heard strange roaring noises coming from Jubilee's shed.

"There's a monster in there!" gasped Bakerloo. "Don't be silly," chuckled Victoria.

The noises were only from Jubilee's new computer game. "It's wicked!" he grinned.

Bakerloo said there *was* a monster in the Underground once. "Cool!" said Jubilee.

Victoria said there was no such thing as monsters and hurried everyone to work.

Millie had just come back from a trip to Australia. "What's this?" asked Ernie.

"It's a didgeridoo, an aboriginal instrument," Millie explained. Ernie peered at it.

Ernie tried to play the didgeridoo while Millie made her train announcements.

The trains heard the noises over the Tannoy. "That's the monster!" said Bakerloo.

The trains decided they must find the monster. "Let's search the tunnels," said City.

Ernie began his rounds and said good morning to Dr Heart. "What's that?" he added.

Dr Heart introduced Fred the skeleton. "I use him to teach my students," he said.

Victoria pulled into the station. Dr Heart had an emergency call and jumped aboard.

"Dr Heart! You've left Fred!" Ernie called, but Victoria's doors shut and she set off.

"I'll just drop you off later, Fred," sighed Ernie. "You can do the rounds with me."

Jubilee thought he heard a monster stamp its feet. "I must tell Bakerloo!" he gasped.

It was just Mr Rails, testing his Bump Flattener. "This will flatten anything!" he said.

"I heard the monster thumping around near the workshop!" Jubilee told Bakerloo.

"It was at International Station only minutes ago," said Bakerloo. "It's a fast mover!"

Bakerloo found Victoria. "Be on your guard," he warned, "for the monster is back!"

"Don't be ridiculous," sniffed Victoria. "It may be on your line!" insisted Bakerloo.

"Monsters, indeed," muttered Victoria, as she ran along. "Stuff and nons – AARGH!"

Victoria had seen Fred the skeleton on Ernie 1 and fled. "Oh, dear," groaned Ernie.

"Help! Help!" Victoria raced along, shrieking. "What's the matter?" asked Millie.

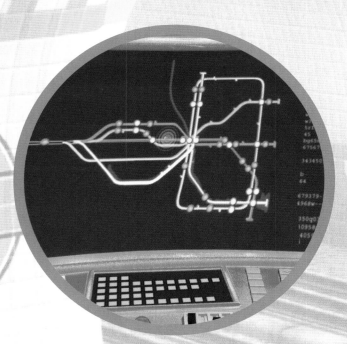

Millie could see that Victoria was shooting round the tracks at an alarming speed.

She called Ernie. "Victoria's going crazy," she said. "You'd better find her quickly."

"Help! Help!" Victoria cried to the others. "There *is* a monster...and it's eaten Ernie!"

The trains were horrified. "This is the saddest day in history," said Bakerloo.

"Oh? Why's that?" asked Ernie.
"Ernie!" cried the trains. "You haven't
been eaten!"

"Of course I haven't," he chuckled. "That
was my friend Fred that Victoria saw."

"The monster ate Fred?" gasped Bakerloo.
"He's a plastic skeleton," Ernie explained.

Ernie was sorry that he had frightened
Victoria. "Oh, I wasn't scared,"
joked Victoria.

"There isn't a monster, then?" asked Circle. "Of course there isn't," replied Ernie.

"But what about the growls?" asked Hammersmith. "And the thumps?" asked Jubilee.

Ernie explained that the noises were a didgeridoo and Mr Rails' Bump Flattener.

"And now," Ernie smiled, "I think you all need to calm down and get some rest."

The trains soon settled down, safe in the knowledge that there was no monster.

"We wouldn't want anything to eat Ernie," said City. "We couldn't do without him!"

Jubilee peeped out of his shed. "Does anyone want to play my monster game with me?" he asked.

"No!" cried the trains. They'd had enough of monsters for one day!

Funny Noises

You may hear a thump,
Or it might be a bump...
You could even hear it tonight.
You may hear a creak,
Or a groan or a squeak,
But don't let it give you a fright!

If you're scared by a knock
Or the tick of a clock,
Don't panic like old Bakerloo –
He heard a strange sound,
Cried, "A monster's around!"
It was only a didgeridoo!

Brave Victoria

Victoria knew all along that there was no such thing as monsters! Use your crayons or pens to colour the bottom picture, using the colours in the top picture to help you.

Passenger Pick-Up Game

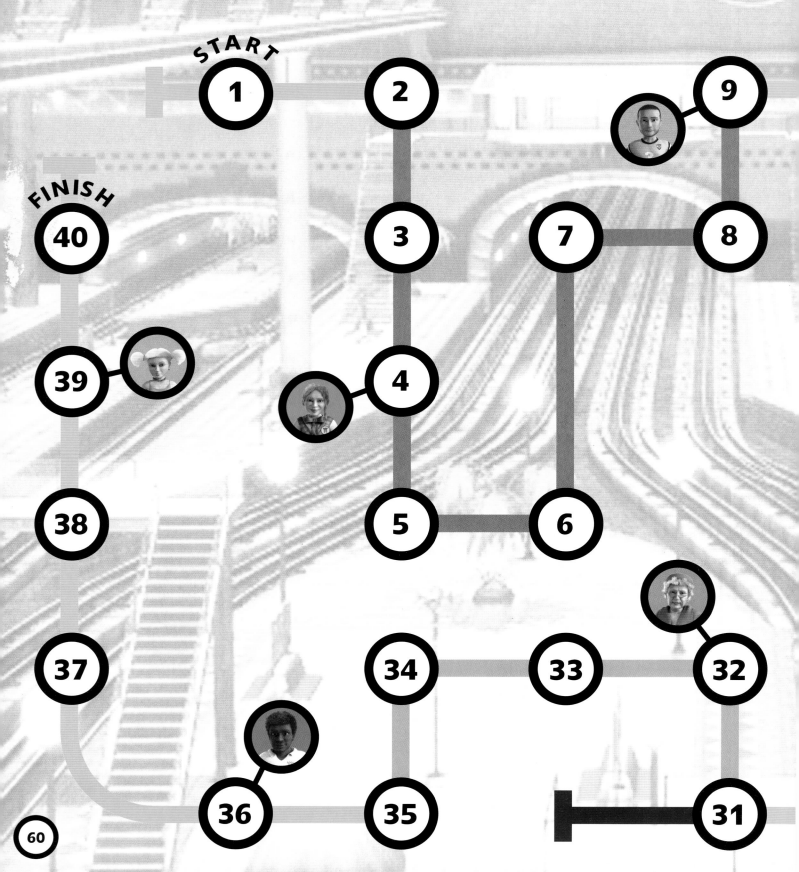

START

1 — 2

9

40 FINISH

3 — 7 — 8

4

39

38

5 — 6

34 — 33 — 32

37

36 — 35   31